Why Leopard Has Spots

WHY LEOPARD HAS SPOTS

Dan Stories from Liberia

Won-Ldy Paye and Margaret H. Lippert
Illustrated by Ashley Bryan

fulcrum kids
Golden, Colorado

First Fulcrum trade paperback edition published February 1999.

Library of Congress Cataloging-in-Publication Data
Paye, Won-Ldy.
     Why Leopard has spots : Dan stories from Liberia / Won-Ldy Paye
and Margaret H. Lippert ; illustrated by Ashley Bryan.
         p.   cm.
     Contents: Why Leopard has spots — Mrs. Chicken and the hungry
crocodile — The talking vegetables — The hunger season — Why
Spider has a big butt — Spider flies to the feast.
     ISBN 1-55591-991-X (paperback)
     ISBN 1-55591-344-X (hardcover)
     1. Tales—Liberia. 2. Dan (African people)—Folklore. [1. Dan
(African people)—Folklore. 2. Folklore—Liberia.] I. Lippert,
Margaret H. II. Bryan, Ashley, ill. III. Title.
PZ8.1.P24Wh   1998
[398.2'096662]—dc21   98-3154
                                CIP
                                AC

The illustrations are linoleum prints.
Book design by Alyssa Pumphrey

The photographs on pages 39 and 41 by Eberhard and Barbara Fischer are published with the permission of the photographers at Museum Rietberg Zürich, Switzerland.

A different version told by the Dan people of the story "Why Leopard Has Spots" entitled "Why Leopard Has Black Spots: A Story from the Dan People of Liberia," told by Won-Ldy Paye and edited by Margaret H. Lippert, was previously published in *Teacher's Read-Aloud Anthology*, Grade 1, Margaret H. Lippert, Anthologist, by Macmillan/McGraw-Hill School Publishing, 1993.

Printed in the United States of America

0 9 8 7 6 5 4 3 2

Fulcrum Publishing
350 Indiana Street, Suite 350
Golden, Colorado 80401-5093
(800) 992-2908 • (303) 277-1623
www.fulcrum-resources.com

Dedicated in memory of my grandmother Gowo,
who loved these stories and gave them to me,
and to the young people who will remember them
and share them with others.
—Won-Ldy Paye

For my husband, Alan,
and our favorite storytellers,
Jocelyn and Dawn.
—Margaret H. Lippert

For a great teacher, my friend,
Sheila Lamb.
—Ashley Bryan

Contents

Acknowledgments

We would like to express our deep appreciation to the many people who helped create this book. To the Dan storytellers who told and preserved the tales. To Margaret Read MacDonald for her help and encouragement from the very beginning. To Laura Kvasnosky, Julie Paschkis, Brenda Guiberson, Linda Kucan, Anne Stribling, Jill Hammond, Melissa Heckler, and Peggy King Anderson for their valuable insights and suggestions, which helped us shape and refine the stories. To Suzanne Barchers, Sara Hanson, Daniel Forrest-Bank, and Cara Hallock for sharing our vision and their editorial expertise. To Ashley Bryan for his stunning illustrations. To Meg's husband, Alan, for his incisive critiques and unerring instinct for cutting to the heart of the stories. To our children, Jocelyn and Dawn Lippert, and Kerlia and Nlorkeahwon Paye, for listening to stories with open hearts and for telling them with humor and love.

Introduction

Babuah! That means "hello" in Dan.

My name is Won-Ldy Paye, pronounced One Day Pay. I grew up in Liberia, a country on the west coast of Africa. Sixteen different ethnic groups live in Liberia, which is about the size of Tennessee. I am a member of the Dan ethnic group. My family lived in a small village of five houses on the outskirts of the town of Tapita in northeastern Liberia.

My playgrounds were the forest around our home, the rice fields my parents farmed, and the river where I fished. Toys and games were everywhere—bamboo sticks were used as juggling rods; holes scooped in the ground and filled with pebbles made *ma kpon,* a counting game; coconut shells with palm leaf sails became boats.

I attended two schools every day. In the mornings I studied reading, writing, and arithmetic—the skills I needed for the world beyond Tapita. In the afternoons I learned drumming, instrument making, dancing, wood carving, mask making, fabric dyeing, and mural painting—the traditional arts and knowledge that nourished and entertained my people.

Before and after school and during school holidays, I worked with my two brothers, my sister, and my many cousins on our family's rice farm. I helped my father clear land and I sowed rice. When the weeds came up, I pulled them for hours in the hot sun. As the rice ripened, I ran around the fields with a stick scaring away hungry birds. During the harvest, I cut the heads of rice off each stalk and tied them into bundles. Then I collected the bundles in baskets and carried them home.

When the butternose fish ran in the river, my friends and I stood waist-deep in the current and held large, round nets to catch them. We often caught enough to share with all our relatives.

If oil was needed for cooking, my brothers and I climbed the tall palm nut trees, cut off clusters of palm nuts, and brought them back to our village. My mother boiled the nuts until they were soft, then we pounded them to release the oil.

After every day's work was done, I listened to the stories my grand-mother told around the fire—stories about the time Spider noticed vegetables were disappearing from his farm, or about the day Spider was invited to a feast and a dance at the same time, or about the morning Hen decided to take her bath in the river. Every night I fell asleep listening to my grandmother's voice.

In Tapita my family are the *tlo ker mehn,* or storytellers, of the Dan community. Other families are known for their carving, their dancing, their drumming, or their singing. Dan wood carvings, masks, and cer-emonial costumes are extremely valuable. You can see them in mu-seums in Europe and the United States. Books have been written about Dan art and culture. But Dan stories have been preserved only within the Dan community. Until recently, no one else had heard them.

From 1980 to 1996 Liberia was torn by civil war. My father and my older brother were killed in the fighting. The rest of my family fled from Tapita to the Ivory Coast. As a result of years of war and displacement, my people and our culture are in peril.

I am the first Dan storyteller who has had the opportunity to leave Liberia and come to the United States. I've continued my *tlo ker mehn* tradition wherever I go, telling our stories to thousands of children and families.

My grandmother died in 1995. She knew I was working on the other side of the world, telling the stories she had told me and preparing them for this book, the first collection of Dan stories ever to be published. She died knowing these stories would live on in the words of storytellers and in the hearts of listeners and readers. As you read and tell them you will be sharing the ancient Dan *tlo ker mehn* heritage and preserving our legacy.

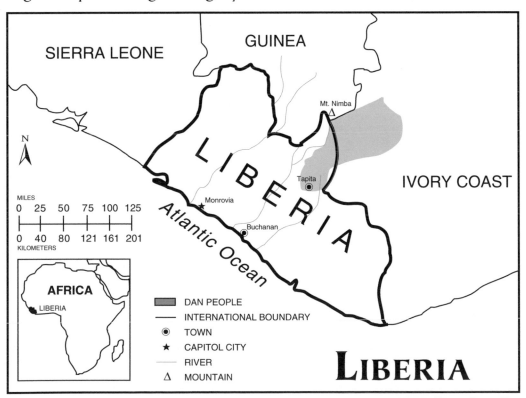

WHY LEOPARD HAS SPOTS

WHY LEOPARD HAS SPOTS

Long ago, in the days when Leopard had a beautiful coat of solid gold, Leopard and Deer were friends. They lived in a little village with Spider, who was a great farmer. Every morning Spider walked to his farm. He worked all day planting, tending, or harvesting his crops. Every evening he cooked a huge meal, and because there was always more than he could eat by himself, he invited his friends Deer and Leopard to dinner.

One day, when Spider was cutting off a head of cabbage, he noticed a space in his row. Someone had taken a cabbage. The next day he noticed an eggplant was gone. Every day another vegetable disappeared from his farm. Sometimes it was a lettuce or several carrots. Other times it was some corn or cassava.

At first Spider didn't care, because he had so much. But when things kept disappearing, he began to get mad.

Spider went to Deer's house and asked, "Have you been stealing vegetables from my farm?"

"Not me!" said Deer. "You invite me to dinner every evening. Why should I steal from you?"

Then Spider asked Leopard, "Have you been stealing from my farm?"

"No!" said Leopard. "You cook such a good dinner for us every evening. I wouldn't steal from you, Spider."

Spider went back home. But every day more of his vegetables disappeared. He got angrier and angrier.

Finally he went back to Deer's house and said, "Please help me find the one who's stealing my vegetables."

"That's easy," Deer said. "Just make a trap. Dig a big hole right inside the gate to your farm. Make a huge fire in the hole, and let it burn down to hot coals. Then cover the hole with dry branches and dead leaves. When the one who's stealing from your farm goes through the gate tonight, the branches will break, and he'll fall into the hole and get burned."

"You are smart," Spider said. "Thank you for your help." Spider hurried to his farm and did exactly what Deer told him to do. Then he went back to his home in the village.

That night, when everyone was sleeping, Deer got up quietly and sneaked out to Spider's farm. He walked carefully around the dry leaves and branches that were covering the hole and stole some cucumbers. He took the cucumbers home and ate them. Then he ran to Leopard's house.

"Leopard," Deer called. "Wake up! Spider wants to see you."

"Where is he?" Leopard asked sleepily.

"On his farm," said Deer.

"Okay," said Leopard. "I'll go, even though it is the middle of the night, because Spider is my friend."

Leopard ran to Spider's farm. Deer followed him quietly. Just inside the gate Leopard stepped on the branches over the hole. The branches broke and Leopard fell WHAM! into the hole. The hot coals burned holes in his coat. "OWWW!" he howled. "Help me!" But no one heard him.

Deer was already on his way to Spider's house. When he got there, he banged on the door. "Spider! Wake up! Come with me! The one who's been stealing your vegetables fell into the trap and is getting burned."

Deer and Spider ran to the farm. Someone was howling with pain. When Spider looked down into the hole and saw his friend Leopard, he was furious. "You lied to me, Leopard," shouted Spider. "Now I see what's going on! You've been stealing all this time!"

"I don't know what you're talking about," Leopard said. "Just help me get out of here!"

Spider reached down and Leopard grabbed his legs. He scrambled out of the hole and rolled in the dirt to put out the flames that were burning holes in his coat.

"I almost burned to death," Leopard cried. "Why did you make a trap? Why did you tell Deer you wanted to see me?"

"Deer told me to make a trap," Spider said. "And I never told him I wanted to see you."

"*You're* the thief, Deer," said Leopard. "And you lied too. Look at me. Because of you, I've got holes all over my beautiful golden coat. You're not my friend anymore. I'm going to eat you up!" Leopard leaped toward Deer, and Deer bounded off into the forest. Leopard raced after him.

Now whenever Leopard sees Deer, he chases him. And since that day, Leopard has black spots all over his beautiful golden coat.

MRS. CHICKEN AND THE HUNGRY CROCODILE

Every morning just before dawn, Mrs. Chicken took her bath in a puddle. One day she was a bit later than usual. The sun peeked over the mountain and lit up her face just as she stepped into the puddle. She noticed her reflection in the water.

"Cluck, cluck," she said, turning her head left and right. "What a pretty chicken I am! Big, bright eyes. Short, smooth beak."

She preened her feathers. "Oh, dear," she moaned. "I can't see my wings. This puddle's too small." She walked down to the river to get a better look.

Mrs. Chicken didn't know that Crocodile lay in the river all day, just underwater, waiting for her next meal. Nor did she know it would be too dark under the trees on the riverbank to see her reflection.

Mrs. Chicken leaned over the water. "Hum," she said. "Where's my beak? I see a long mouth and sharp teeth."

She flapped her wings. "Where are my wings? I see legs and green skin."

Crocodile saw Mrs. Chicken looking down at her. She lay very still. She was hungry. She waited.

"When I look at myself in the river," Mrs. Chicken said, "I look different." Just to make sure, she moved to one side. Crocodile moved, too. Then Mrs. Chicken moved to the other side. So did Crocodile.

"Yes, it's me," Mrs. Chicken said. She stepped into the river.

SNAP! Crocodile grabbed Mrs. Chicken's foot in her mouth.

"BOK!" said Mrs. Chicken. "Let go!"

Crocodile dragged Mrs. Chicken to her house on an island in the middle of the river. She slammed the door with her tail. Then she opened her mouth. Mrs. Chicken flew up to the rafters.

"Come down," Crocodile said. "I'm going to eat you up."

"*Me?*" Mrs. Chicken squawked. "You can't eat me."

"Oooh, yes I can," said Crocodile. "And I will."

"But … ," said Mrs. Chicken, "you shouldn't eat me."

"Why not?" asked Crocodile.

"Because," said Mrs. Chicken, "I'm your *sister.*"

Crocodile laughed. "You're not my sister. You have speckled feathers. I have green scales. You have wings. I don't. You have a beak. I have a mouth with sharp teeth. And these teeth," Crocodile opened her mouth wide, "are going to *eat you now!*"

"No!" said Mrs. Chicken. "We look different, but we're sisters. I'll prove it. Just give me a little time."

"All right," chuckled Crocodile. "In the meantime, I'll fatten you up. The longer I wait, the plumper you'll get."

Crocodile yawned and stretched out beside her eggs. Soon she was snoring.

Mrs. Chicken made her nest in the corner opposite Crocodile. Then she settled down to lay her own eggs.

Every day Crocodile gave Mrs. Chicken grain to eat. Mrs. Chicken got fatter and fatter. Crocodile got hungrier and hungrier.

One evening Crocodile said, "Tomorrow I am going to eat you. Mmm."

"We'll see," said Mrs. Chicken. She waited until Crocodile was sleeping. Then she carefully put her eggs beside Crocodile. She took Crocodile's eggs to her own nest.

Just before dawn, the eggs started to hatch. Crocodile woke up.

"Mrs. Chicken!" Crocodile called. "Wake up! My babies are hatching … but they have silly little beaks … and funny little wings … like yours!"

"My eggs are hatching, too," said Mrs. Chicken. "Look!" She moved off her nest.

"Oh," said Crocodile. "What beautiful babies you have … what gorgeous green scales … what lovely long mouths … like mine."

"I told you," said Mrs. Chicken. "We *are* sisters! You almost *ate* me! Your own *sister!*"

"I'm really sorry, Sister Chicken," said Crocodile.

"I have an idea," said Mrs. Chicken. "Since you like my babies, why don't you take them? I'll take your funny-looking babies."

"Thank you, Sister Chicken," said Crocodile.

"Don't mention it," said Mrs. Chicken. "Sisters help one another." So they switched babies.

"Time for us to go home now." Mrs. Chicken said. She and her babies climbed onto Crocodile's back, and Crocodile took them across the river.

"Bye, Sister," Crocodile said.

Mrs. Chicken waved her wing and hurried her chicks up the riverbank. "Come along, children. Cluck, cluck!"

"See you next time," called Crocodile.

"There won't be a next time," called Mrs. Chicken as she disappeared through the trees. "I tricked you." She laughed. "We aren't really sisters after all!"

From that day on, Mrs. Chicken and her children never go near the river, and they always take their baths in puddles. "Big enough," Mrs. Chicken tells her children. "And *much* too small for crocodiles!"

THE TALKING VEGETABLES

BAM! BAM! BAM!

"Who's pounding on my door so early in the morning?" Spider shouted.

"Your neighbors. Time to clear the land for our village farm."

"Go away," said Spider. "I'm tired."

"But we need you," they said. "If everyone helps, there will be enough vegetables for all of us."

Spider yawned. "I have plenty of rice. I don't need your vegetables."

Everyone in the village walked down the road to a clearing in the forest. Everyone except Spider. They worked all day cutting down bushes, tearing out vines, and digging up roots. They raked smooth beds and built a waterway.

The next morning, the people came again to Spider's door.

BAM! BAM! BAM!

"Who's there?" Spider called.

"Your neighbors. Come help us plant the seeds."

"I said no, and I meant no. Now go away," said Spider.

The villagers carried seeds to the farm and planted them in straight rows. They planted cassava, tomato, squash, pumpkin, cabbage, cucumber, pepper, and many different kinds of beans and greens.

A month later, Spider's neighbors knocked on his door again.

BAM! BAM! BAM!

Spider opened his door and shouted, "What do you want now?"

"Time to weed the farm," they answered.

"I didn't help before, and I'm not helping now," Spider said. He slammed the door and went back to bed.

All day the people pulled weeds. Their knees hurt, their backs ached, and their hands were sore.

In time, the vegetables began to ripen. The villagers picked what they wanted. Anybody who needed food went to the farm.

One day Spider said to himself, "I'm getting tired of rice. Plain rice, day after day after day. I live here. I'm part of this village too. I'm going to pick myself some vegetables to go with my rice."

When he got to the farm he couldn't believe his eyes. Huge cucumbers lay on the ground. Giant pumpkins rested under green leaves. Juicy tomatoes hung from vines.

"Wow!" said Spider. "Those tomatoes look delicious. I'll just take one, or maybe two."

Spider went through the gate and reached out to pick a tomato from the nearest plant. The tomato shook itself and said, "What are you doing?"

Spider said, "Wha … ? A talking tomato?"

The tomato said, "Why do you think you can pick me when you didn't come to clear the land or plant my seeds or pull the weeds? Get out of here!"

Spider backed away. He looked around and said, "There are so many fat cucumbers on that vine. I'll just take one, or maybe two."

But as he walked toward the cucumber vine, it started moving away from him. Spider was surprised. He'd never seen a moving vine before. The vine twisted all over the ground. "You can't pick us," said a cucumber. "You didn't clear the land. You didn't plant our seeds. You didn't pull the weeds."

Spider ran to the other side of the farm. Ahead he saw a perfect pumpkin—big enough, but not too big. "I'll grab that pumpkin on my way out of the farm," he said. But he couldn't lift it. The pumpkin stuck to the ground. He tugged and pulled, but the pumpkin wouldn't move. "You can't take me," the pumpkin said. "You didn't help make the farm. Go away."

Spider tried to find his way out of the farm, but the vegetables reached up to grab him. Leaves covered his eyes. Stems stretched out to trip him. Spider staggered toward the gate and ran all the way back to the village. When he got home he was tired and hungry.

That night, and every night after that, he put a pot of water over the fire, boiled some rice, and ate the rice for dinner. Plain rice.

THE HUNGER SEASON

Day after day it rained. The fields and gardens were flooded. There was no more food in the village, and everyone was hungry. It was the hunger season.

People went deep into the jungle to search for food, often staying there for two or three days. Sometimes even then they couldn't find anything to eat.

Spider was hungry. He went to his friend Torli and said, "Let's go hunting together. Maybe we'll find something to eat if we both look. Then we can share what we find." Torli agreed.

The next morning they set out. They walked and walked, but they didn't see anything to eat. Finally they came to a river. Spider said, "Let's go fishing. Maybe we'll catch a nice big butternose fish."

They wove a long fishing net out of palm leaves and started wading up the river, dragging the net between them. They went far upriver, but they didn't catch anything. Then they waded downriver. All they caught was one tiny shrimp.

"This isn't much," said Torli, "but half a shrimp is better than nothing." They made a fire and boiled some water.

While the shrimp cooked, Spider thought, *That shrimp isn't much for two people to share. After I eat my half I'll still be hungry. Maybe I can trick Torli into giving me the next thing we find, which will surely be bigger than the shrimp.*

"Torli," he said, "This shrimp is too small for us to share. You can eat the shrimp, and I will eat the next thing we find."

"All right," Torli said.

Spider was delighted. His plan was working perfectly. Torli ate the whole shrimp while Spider watched.

They looked all day for food, and Spider got hungrier and hungrier. Toward evening they found a hummingbird nest with one tiny egg.

"It's not fair," Spider grumbled.

"Why not?" asked Torli. "You can eat the egg, because I had the shrimp. I'll stick to our agreement."

Spider said, "This hummingbird egg is even smaller than the shrimp. You should eat the hummingbird egg too. Then the next two things will be mine."

Torli said, "Well, okay. If you think that's more fair, we'll do that." So Torli boiled the egg and ate it. It was small, but at least it was something.

The next day they went farther into the forest and still couldn't find anything to eat. Just as they were about to turn back, they saw an eagle's nest at the top of a tree. A baby eaglet poked its head out of the nest. The mama eagle was nowhere in sight.

"That's mine!" shouted Spider. "I can get that eaglet easily. He's too young to fly." The eaglet would make a good meal, much better than the shrimp and the hummingbird egg put together. He climbed up the tree, hand over hand. Spider could see the nest just above him. He was thinking how smart he was. But just as Spider reached into the nest, the mama eagle plummeted out of the sky and grabbed Spider in her talons.

"Help, help!" Spider screamed, but there was nothing Torli could do. Eagle soared over to the river and dropped Spider. He landed on the sandy bank.

Spider was stunned. The next thing he knew, Torli was shaking him and calling, "Are you all right, Spider?"

Spider sat up and moved his arms and legs. "I'm lucky I landed on this soft sand," he said. "It saved my life." He got up slowly and started back to the village with Torli. Then he saw something in the reeds that took his breath away. It was the top of a huge shining ostrich egg. The bottom was buried in the sand. Torli turned to see what Spider was looking at.

"Don't touch that egg," Spider said. "Don't even look at it. I lost the eaglet, but this egg is mine. We made an agreement that the next two things we found would be mine, remember?"

"Yes," said Torli sadly. He was disappointed, but he had to stick with his word.

"This egg is too big to boil," Spider said. "I'll have to roast it right where it is, in its shell." Spider built a huge fire around the egg.

Spider told Torli, "This egg is all mine. Go far away where you can't even smell it. I want to eat it all by myself." So Torli walked far off and sat down all by himself.

After a while, Spider said, "I guess my egg is ready now." He let the fire die down and the egg cool off. He found a sharp rock so he could break the shell. Torli heard a loud CRACK. Spider shouted, "Oh, no!"

"What happened, Spider?" Torli called. "Isn't it done yet?"

"Look!" Spider cried. Torli came running. The eggshell was empty. The baby ostrich had hatched long ago and walked away, leaving only the top of its shell in the sand. Spider had nothing to eat.

Since that day, Spider always shares what he has, even when it is very, very small.

to the FEAST...to the DANCE

WHY SPIDER HAS A BIG BUTT

Spider couldn't decide where he wanted to live. "Come live in the mountains with me," said his friend Dantay. He put his arm around Spider's plump waist.

"Come live in my village by the river," said his friend Layva. She smiled at Spider.

"We have great dance festivals in the mountains," said Dantay, "and you love to dance."

"We have great feasts by the river," said Layva, "and you love to eat."

"I guess I'll live right in the middle," said Spider. "When you have a festival, I'll go up to your village and dance," he said to Dantay.

"And when we have a feast, come down to our village and eat!" said Layva.

Spider was happy. He loved to dance, and he loved to eat. He built himself a beautiful home in the forest halfway between the mountains and the river. He could go up to the dances, and he could go down to the feasts. He wouldn't have to miss anything.

The next week Dantay came to visit. "We are having a dance on Saturday," he said. "Can you come?"

"Oh, sure," said Spider. "But I might not hear the drums way out here. I'll tie this long rope around my waist. You take the end of the rope up to your village. When the drumming begins, pull the rope. Then I'll know when to come." So Spider tied the rope around his waist and gave the end to Dantay.

That afternoon Layva came to visit. "Spider, you are invited to a feast in our village on Saturday."

"Oh, no," said Spider. "I'm going to Dantay's dance festival on Saturday. I don't want to miss that."

"Come to the feast first," said Layva. "Then go and dance when you are full."

"But the festival might be over by the time I get there," said Spider. "Maybe I should go to the dance first and get really hungry, and then come to the feast."

"But the food might be all gone by then," said Layva.

Spider thought for a moment. "I know!" he said. "I'll tie another rope around my waist. If you pull first, I'll go to the feast first and then to the dance. If Dantay pulls first, I'll go to the dance first and then to the feast. That way I won't miss anything!" So Spider tied another rope around his waist and gave the end to Layva.

On Saturday Spider woke up early. "A dance and a feast on the same day!" he said. He sat down to wait. The sun rose higher and higher in the sky.

"What's the matter with them?" Spider wondered. "Why doesn't anyone pull? I don't want to miss the food. I'd better go to the feast." He took a few steps down toward the river and paused.

"Wait a minute," he said to himself. "If I get there and the food isn't ready yet, I'll miss all the dancing. I'd better go to the festival first." He took a few steps up the mountain. Then he stopped. "But if the dance festival hasn't begun yet, and the feast has started without me, I might get to the feast after all the food is gone."

Spider didn't know what to do. He sat down to think. At that moment, the feast was ready and the dance began. Dantay and Layva both pulled their ropes at the same time.

"Aggg!" screamed Spider. "Stop! Stop! Stop!" But no one heard him.

Dantay and Layva wondered why the rope didn't give.

Maybe it's stuck on a rock, thought Dantay.

Maybe it's twisted around a tree, thought Layva.

They pulled harder and harder. Spider's nice plump waist was being squeezed tighter and tighter. He could hardly breathe. He felt something swelling under him. Something very, very big.

"Help," he whispered. "Help meee … aghhh." At the same moment, Dantay and Layva both gave one last huge jerk on the rope. Spider's legs buckled under him and he crumpled to the ground. He couldn't move.

I guess Spider must have gone to the feast, thought Dantay.

I guess Spider must have gone to the dance, thought Layva.

They both dropped their ropes at the same time.

Spider gulped breaths of air. "Now … I can't go … to the festival … or the feast," he moaned. "And what is that huge lump under me?" He looked down. He poked it with one leg. "Oh, no," he groaned. "It's part of me."

Then he poked it with another leg. "Yes," he said sadly, "it's really me. Now I have a tiny waist and a big, huge butt."

And that's the way Spider has been ever since.

Spider Flies to the Feast

Spider and Dog were friends. Every day Spider would float downriver to visit Dog. But he always had to walk home. No one could swim upstream against the swift current.

Spider loved to play tricks on Dog. One day he said, "I have a new trick. I can go home without walking on the ground! Can you do that?"

Dog scratched his neck with his hind leg. Scratching always helped him think. "No," he said, as his leg hit the ground with a thump, "and neither can you."

"Yes, I can," said Spider. "I can walk in space."

Dog laughed. "Nobody can walk in space," he said.

"Nobody *except* me," said Spider.

"Prove it," said Dog.

Spider climbed to the top of Dog's house. He let out a silky thread so thin that Dog couldn't see it. Then he waved one leg.

"Let go," said Dog. "You aren't walking through space. Anybody can wave a leg out in space."

Spider waved another leg, and another, and another. He was waiting for the wind.

"Let go with *all* your legs," said Dog.

The wind came up. It blew the end of the thread toward Spider's house, and the thread caught on Spider's roof. Then Spider stepped off Dog's roof onto the thread and began to walk.

"How do you do that?" asked Dog. "I never saw anybody walk in space before." He followed Spider all the way to his house.

Spider climbed down from his roof and grinned. "Did you like my trick?" he asked.

"You were lucky, Spider. You could have crashed and hurt your-self. Tricks can really get you in trouble. So from now on, no more tricks." Dog wagged his tail good-bye and jumped into the river. He floated home with the current.

The next day Spider floated downriver to see Dog again. "I have a better trick," he said. "I can get home without walking on the ground or walking in space."

"How?" Dog asked.

"On the river," said Spider.

Dog scratched behind his left ear. Then he shook his head. "The current is too fast," said Dog. "No one can go upriver."

"I can," said Spider.

"Prove it," said Dog.

Spider took a deep breath and plunged into the river. He sank below the surface. Dog bounded to the edge of the riverbank to res-cue his friend, but stopped short as Spider's head bobbed up.

"Watch carefully," Spider called. He began moving all eight legs at once, very fast, skating on the surface of the water. Gradually he worked his way upstream.

Dog was amazed. He raced up the path and waited by Spider's house. Soon Spider skated to the bank and climbed out. "Did you like my new trick?" he asked.

"How did you do that?" asked Dog. "I never saw anybody walk on water before. That's dangerous, Spider. You could have drowned. I told you that tricks can really get you in trouble. So no more tricks." Dog jumped in the river and floated downstream.

Spider waved a dripping leg and called, "Tomorrow I will come visit you without walking on the ground, without walking in space, and without skating on the river."

When Dog got to his house he waded out of the river and shook himself dry. Then he sat down and scratched his belly. "That spider! What will he do next?" Dog wondered.

Early the next morning, Spider cooked a huge pumpkin, cut off the lid, scooped out the seeds, spiced it up, climbed inside, and pulled the lid shut. *Soon Dog will get tired of waiting for me,* he thought. *He'll come looking for me and when he sees this yummy pumpkin he'll carry it back to his house, with me inside it!* Spider was so excited he could hardly sit still.

Dog waited and waited for Spider. The sun rose high in the sky, but still Spider didn't come. *I wonder what happened to Spider,* Dog thought. *Maybe this time his trick got him in trouble. Maybe he's hurt.*

Dog trotted up the path to look for Spider. As he got close to Spider's house, he smelled something delicious. *Mmmm,* he thought. *Lunch time.*

When he rounded the bend he saw the pumpkin in the middle of the yard. *Yum!* he thought. *That's enough food for both of us.*

"Spider!" he called. "Where are you?"

Spider heard Dog calling him, but he didn't answer. *I'll wait until Dog gets this pumpkin back to his house, then I'll answer him,* Spider thought. *Won't he be surprised!* Spider had to cover his mouth with three legs so Dog wouldn't hear him laughing.

Hmmm, thought Dog. *I guess I missed Spider. He must be up to one of his tricks. I'll just take a little taste of this pumpkin to make sure it's ready.* He sank his teeth into the pumpkin and bit Spider's leg.

"Ouch!" yelled Spider.

Oh, dear, thought Dog, glancing around, *Spider must be hurt. I'd better go look for him, But this pumpkin is so good. I'll just take one more bite before I go.* Dog took another big bite of pumpkin and almost bit Spider's leg off completely.

"Stop biting me!" cried Spider. He crawled out of the pumpkin, rubbing his injured leg.

"What were you doing in there?" asked Dog.

"Waiting for you to carry me to your house," said Spider.

Dog cocked his head to one side. "*That* was your trick?" he asked.

"Yes," said Spider sadly.

"That was really stupid," said Dog. "I could have eaten you up by accident. I told you: Tricks can really get you in trouble."

Spider limped to the river and put his hurt leg in the cool water. "All right, Dog," he said. "From now on, no more tricks."

For many months Spider remembered what he had said to Dog. Of course he kept thinking of great tricks, but he didn't play them on anybody.

Then the dry season came. Day after day the sun hung high and hot in the sky. Spider swung lazily from a thread, dangling his legs, trying to catch a breeze. This was long ago, when Spider didn't have bent legs.

Spider saw Eagle stretch her wings and soar high into the sky. "It's cool here," Eagle called to the other birds. "Come on up." Spider watched as the sky filled with birds. Some swooped in huge circles, and some flitted in sharp zigzags.

The Great Spirit looked down from her home high above the clouds. She loved watching the birds zoom and glide. "I would like to reward you for entertaining me," she said. "Come to my house to-morrow for a feast."

Spider heard the Great Spirit. *That's not fair,* he thought. *Why shouldn't I go too? I'm better than those birds. I have eight legs. Birds only have two.* He waved his legs proudly, but no one was watching.

Spider squinted up into the sky. "I know!" he said. "I'll make my own wings and fly to the feast myself!"

Spider pranced over to Quail's nest. "Do you have some extra feathers around?"

"You can have the ones over there in the grass," she said.

"Thank you," said Spider.

Then he called to Eagle, "Could I borrow some feathers?"

"Take the ones on the ground below my nest," she called.

Spider asked Vulture, Woodpecker, and Blue Heron for feathers. He got big, strong feathers. Then he asked Pepper Bird, Parrot, and Hummingbird. He got small, fluffy feathers. He got feathers from every kind of bird. Soon he had a huge pile of feathers—long and short, wide and thin, and all the colors of the rainbow. He arranged them on the ground in the shape of a coat with wings.

Now I need some glue, Spider thought. With a sharp rock he scraped the bark of a rubber tree until sticky white gum seeped out. He spread this on the feathers.

When the glue was dry he put on his new coat and flapped his legs. His wings flopped back and forth. After bumping along on the ground for a few moments, he took off into the air. At first he wobbled shakily from side to side, but soon he began to soar smoothly. His wings lifted him higher and higher. "I'm flying!" he shouted. "Wait till the birds see this!"

The next day the birds were all up early. They started flying to the feast. Spider woke up late. He poked his head out of his door and saw them high in the sky. "Hey, wait for me," he called. But no one heard him. Spider hurried into his winged coat and took off after them. "Here I come!" he cried.

All morning Spider flew. He followed the birds into the clouds. His legs ached. His back hurt. And he was hungry. Finally he arrived at the feast.

The Great Spirit was talking. "Welcome. I hope you all enjoy the feast I have prepared for you today," she said. Spider settled into a corner and eyed the food spread out on the table. The birds were listening carefully to the Great Spirit. None of them noticed him. "This is the first time you have all been together, so before we eat I would like you to introduce yourselves to one another."

Eagle preened her feathers. "My name is Eagle."

Parrot squawked, "My name is Parrot."

Hummingbird hovered near the Great Spirit and announced, "I am Hummingbird." The Great Spirit smiled and held out her hand. Hummingbird alighted on the open palm and folded her wings.

After all the birds had introduced themselves, the Great Spirit pointed to Spider. "I see we have a guest," she said. "What is your name?"

Oh, no, Spider thought. *I wasn't expecting this. If I say Spider the birds will throw me out.* He staggered to his feet and shook his wings to give himself a few moments to think. *I have feathers from all the birds here, so I know what I'll say.*

"My name is All of You," said Spider.

The Great Spirit nodded. "Now that the introductions are finished," she said, "it is time to eat."

Hummingbird flitted over to a bright red hibiscus. Parrot cracked some sunflower seeds. Pepper Bird plucked a sweet pepper off a vine.

"Wait!" shouted Spider. The birds froze. "Great Spirit," asked Spider, "who is this feast for?"

The Great Spirit leaned forward. "This feast is for all of you," she said.

"Wow!" Spider said, spreading his wings and pushing the birds aside. He flapped up onto the table and shouted, "This feast is just for me, 'cause my name is All of You. You can't eat *any* of my food."

He snatched the flower from Hummingbird. He gobbled up Parrot's seeds. He shoved the pepper into his mouth.

The birds shrieked and hooted and honked, but Spider was fast. In a flash all the food was gone. Spider had eaten up every bit all by himself.

The Great Spirit saw that the birds were angry. *Spider will be sorry,* she thought.

When it was time for them to leave, Eagle turned to Hummingbird and said, "Those little tail feathers on All of You look a lot like yours."

"Yes, they *are* mine," Hummingbird said. "And those long feathers on his wings look a lot like yours. All of You must really be Spider."

"Whoops," said Spider. "I think I heard my name. I'd better go now." Spider took off for home.

Eagle soared after him and said, "Spider, you tricked us. I want my feathers back."

"Oh, sure," said Spider. "I have plenty more." He broke off Eagle's feathers and gave them to her.

Next, Pepper Bird glided over and took back his feathers. Then Goose, and Turkey, and Parrot. After that all the birds came. One by one they took their feathers from Spider.

Spider flapped his legs, but he didn't go up. He began to fall. *I can't slow down,* he realized. *What am I going to do now?* Just then Hummingbird flew by.

"Help me, little Hummingbird," Spider said, "Hurry down to earth. Tell my family to cover the ground under me with soft leaves."

But Hummingbird remembered what Spider had done. She was hungry, and she knew her friends were too. She sped down to earth and called Spider's family. "Spider has a new trick he wants to show you! Bring thorny branches and stick them in the ground with the points straight up. Spider will stop just above them."

Spider's family was used to his tricks. They did exactly as Hummingbird said.

Spider fell through the clouds. He heard everybody clapping and cheering, "Hey, Spider! Come on, Spider! Show us your new trick!"

"What's wrong with you?" Spider yelled. "Where are the soft leaves? Why are there sharp bran … "

THWOK!

Poor Spider lay on the thorns. He could hardly move. The only thing that saved his life was the hard glue from the bird feather coat. All his legs were broken, and that is why Spider's legs are crooked.

Spider still loves to fly, but he never again tried to make wings. Now he has to wait for the wind so he can sail through the air on his silken thread.

About the Stories

I learned all the stories in this collection from my grandmother, Gowo. All of them are traditional stories of the Dan people, told by parents and grandparents. In this way the stories have been preserved not in books, but in people's memories.

Details in the stories change each time they are told, but particular stories are recognizable by special characters or events. In the Dan culture, stories are not usually referred to by their titles. Someone just begins telling a story. After the first few words the listeners know which tale they will hear: for example, "Long ago, in the days when Leopard had a beautiful coat of solid gold … ." They look forward to how the story will be different from other versions they have heard. Each time they hope it will be more entertaining than ever before. Their interest and curiosity challenge each teller to be funnier and more dramatic.

In Dan stories, animals have human thoughts and feelings. They often act as people do. One important character, Spider, appears in many Dan stories. Spider is similar to the familiar spider character, Anansi, of the Ashanti people from Ghana.

Why Leopard Has Spots

I remember my grandmother telling us "Why Leopard Has Spots" many times when I was 5 or 6 years old. This was her way of letting us know that it's important for us to get along with one another in our family. The story teaches us we shouldn't act like Deer.

Stories in the Dan culture take the place of rules. When I was a little older and saw younger children having a problem, I'd tell them a story related to the problem so they could work it out themselves. We didn't talk about who was right and who was wrong, about who was taking things that weren't theirs or who was lying. The stories did the teaching. Everybody could save face.

Mrs. Chicken and the Hungry Crocodile

Some Dan stories are told simply for entertainment. "Mrs. Chicken and the Hungry Crocodile" doesn't have a moral. It just tells why things are they way they are.

I first heard this story from my grandmother when I was very young. The way she told it, it was just a short little story.

When I was about 12 or 13 years old and working on our farm, my friends and I would take a break and tell stories just to make each other laugh. We'd all try to remember stories our grandmothers had told us from the "libraries" in our heads, then we'd try to tell these stories in a funnier way. It was a competition to see who could tell the funniest story.

My younger brother Won-Yen told "Mrs. Chicken and the Hungry Crocodile" at one of these competitions. It was so funny that I always tell this story the way he told it that day.

The Talking Vegetables

"The Talking Vegetables," like "Why Leopard Has Spots," is a story with a moral, but it's a different kind of moral. It's about what you should do, not about what you shouldn't do.

In an African village everybody has a responsibility. If you are a small child, your task will be small; if you are big, it will be big.

My grandmother used to tell us this story when we were working together on our farm. But because it was hot and I was tired, I'd only remember bits and pieces. So she'd tell us the same stories in the evening, when we were relaxed. "The Talking Vegetables" is one of the stories she told us to help us understand that everyone in the family has to do his or her part.

In addition to our own farms, every Dan community has a village farm, like the farm in "The Talking Vegetables." Everyone in the village works on this farm, and everyone shares the vegetables. If somebody gets sick, friends pick vegetables from the village farm for the family. When we have an important celebration, we sell vegetables from the village farm to buy what we need for the festival. Everyone works hard to make the community farm a village treasure.

The Hunger Season

"The Hunger Season" is one of the stories people tell when their stomachs are full. You'll never hear "The Hunger Season" when people are hungry. It's a popular story during the harvest season, when we can laugh about our hardships because they are over for another year.

Spider reminds us of ourselves, because, like Spider, sometimes we don't have enough food to eat. Because we don't tell stories about ourselves, we use Spider.

In Tapita the harvest season is from November to January. February through April is the planting season, when we prepare the fields and sow the seeds. We have a long growing season that starts in May, when the rains begin.

The hunger season occurs in September and October, at the peak of the rainy season, when it rains so heavily that we can't work on the farm. The vegetables won't be ripe for another month or two so food is scarce—there aren't even any vegetables for sale in the market. Each family has so little to eat that we all really have to share. Every Dan child remembers the hunger seasons.

WHY SPIDER HAS A BIG BUTT

One day my grandmother was teaching us how to weave baskets. Before the real weaving lesson began she told us "Why Spider Has a Big Butt." The story provided the foundation for the weaving lesson. "If you want to weave a basket," she told us, "do it step by step. First you have to go out and cut palm leaf branches in the forest and rattan vines in the swamp."

When we brought the branches and vines back to the village, she showed us how to pull the stringy fibers off the backs of the palm leaves and twist the fibers into long ropes. Then she taught us how to chop the leaves off the rattan vines, split the vines into thin strips, and soak the strips to make them soft. When everything was ready, she showed us how to weave. "Don't start weaving until you have everything ready," she said, "because if you don't do things in order you'll end up with nothing, like Spider."

Dan children are taught that each skill has to be done step by step. We learn to finish one thing, then go on to the next. If Spider had realized this, he could have gone to the dance and told his friends he would come to the feast when he was finished dancing. He could have had everything, but because he wanted everything at once, he had nothing.

Once we'd heard "Why Spider Has a Big Butt" one sentence was enough to remind us what we should do. If my grandmother saw me pounding rice, cooking soup, and at the same time running back and forth behind the house to play, she might say, "You're going to have a big butt like Spider!"

Spider Flies to the Feast

"Spider Flies to the Feast" is the kind of story Dan people say has "no head and no tail" because it can go on forever, with one story leading to another and then another. A lot of times when a young child hears stories like these he goes to sleep before the end.

The first section of "Spider Flies to the Feast" is a story about Spider and Dog. Every time we told this story we'd think of more tricks Spider played on Dog. We'd just make them up. Sometimes we'd think of tricks Dog could play on Spider too. We'd all try to make our story funnier than the one told before.

Sometimes this kind of story was told by lots of us together. When someone ran out of ideas he could pass the story on to someone else. That person could add more tricks or just end it. It always ends the same way: "Spider decided not to play any more tricks"—until the next story when Spider starts playing tricks again.

In the second section the Great Spirit invites the birds to a feast. In the Dan culture we have many spirits, but the most important one is the Great Spirit. When a feast was announced by the Great Spirit, all the birds knew it would be a very special event.

Although I first heard this story from my grandmother, it was funnier when my Aunt Gbandeh, who was my mother's sister, told it to us. My aunt's version is the one I always tell now.

I remember my aunt describing Spider as he was falling, looking at the ground and saying, "Wow! What is going to happen to me when I get there?" Then she asked us, "What do *you* think will happen to Spider?"

My aunt always interrupted her stories with questions like this to engage us in the story and get our attention. The story swung back and forth between teller and listeners. Everyone laughed—at the story, at the teller, and at themselves. In a Dan village storytelling always is interrupted with laughing because we all enjoy playing with stories.

Glossary

Anansi (ah-nan´-see): A trickster character who sometimes appears as a man and sometimes as a spider. Anansi is the hero of many Ashanti folktales. He usually tricks other animals or people, though sometimes he falls into his own trap.

Ashanti (ah-shan´-tee): The largest ethnic group living in Ghana. Most Ashanti are farmers who raise crops such as cacao seeds, which are used to make cocoa and chocolate. Ashanti weavers are famous for producing colorful cloth with complicated, detailed patterns.

Babuah (bah-boo´-ah): Means "good morning" or "hello" in the Dan language.

Balaphone (bal´-ah-fone): An instrument of dried hollow gourds with wooden strips on top, similar to a xylophone. The gourds and wooden strips are arranged in order by size and are tied together with vines or rope. The strips are hit with wooden mallets that are often tipped with rubber to soften the sound.

Butternose fish: Orange fish that have unusual translucent noses. Butternose fish are plump, oily, and tasty. They swim in groups, usually traveling upstream during the rainy season when the streams are full.

Cassava (kah-sah´-vah): A small tropical shrub with thick roots, which are eaten like potatoes. Cassava, an important source of starch, is eaten with vegetables, fruits, and fish to provide a balanced diet.

Dan: An ethnic group of about 350,000 people living in the forests of the Nimba Mountain Range in northeastern Liberia and western Ivory Coast. They are farmers who grow rice, cassava, and vegetables. In addition to these foods, they eat fish which they catch in streams and rivers. They grow coffee and rubber to sell. The Dan are famous for their artistic accomplishments

Gbandeh (gben´-deh): The sister of Won-Ldy's mother, who was always referred to as Mami Gbandeh because she had 8 children. A woman with many children is deeply respected in the Dan culture, and is often called "Mami" even by children who are not her own. Mami Gbandeh was a fine storyteller. She owned a large rubber plantation and was an excellent farmer. She was a very unusual woman because she was a wife, a mother, and an entrepreneur.

Ghana (ga´-na): A country in West Africa east of Liberia, separated from Liberia by the Ivory Coast.

Gowo (go-wo): Won-Ldy's grandmother. Gowo had many talents. She was an herbalist who could set broken bones and heal other injuries; she was an excellent weaver who made beautiful baskets, mats, and fishing nets; and she was also a great *tlo ker mehn*. Won-Ldy remembers her in her 80s as a quiet and peaceful person who often sat watching her grandchildren without saying anything but noticing everything. When she performed stories she became a totally different person. She took on the quality of each character and brought every story to life. She was responsible for educating the members of her family in the *tlo ker mehn* tradition.

Great Spirit: Peace and order in Dan communities are maintained by the elders. Even the town chief is selected by the elders and is answerable to them. The elders stay in power by calling upon spirits from the forest, which appear in the village from time to time in masks and body-concealing costumes. The Dan believe that these spirits are descended from their ancestors. Weavers have their spirit, as do potters and hunters and farmers and wood carvers. These spirits help them to do their best. In Tapita the most important spirit is the Great Spirit. She is portrayed by someone in a mask with female features, a feathered headdress, a bulky raffia skirt, and a huge white shawl. She comes into the village to resolve serious problems or to announce decisions that affect the whole village, like when and where to hunt, when to plant, and where to have burials. If an ordinary person were to announce such decisions, people might grumble and not obey them, but every Dan person accepts the authority of the Great Spirit without question.

The Great Spirit in a Dan village.

Hunger Season: The time of the heaviest rains, during September and October, before the harvest, when the food stored from the previous year is running low.

Liberia: Africa's oldest republic. The name *Liberia* means "land of the free." Freed American slaves settled along the coast beginning in the early 1800s. Liberia's Constitution, written in 1847, was modeled after the U.S. Constitution. Liberia is about the same size and shape as Tennessee. Its southern border stretches 370 miles (595 kilometers) along the Atlantic Ocean. North of the narrow coastal plain, heavily forested mountains rising 4,500 feet (1,372 meters) are cut by 15 major rivers. The climate is hot, with an average temperature of 80°F (27°C), and humid (the rainy season lasts from April to October).

Ma kpon (ma kpo): A Dan counting game similar to the game known in other parts of Africa as *serata, owari, wari, awari,* or *mankala.* Archaeologists have found games resembling *ma kpon* that existed 5,000 years ago in Africa. They think these games may originally have been used for record-keeping systems or in religious ceremonies. *Ma kpon* is very popular with Dan men and women, but children enjoy playing it too. The game board has 12 round holes arranged in 2 parallel rows of 6. Dan game boards are beautifully carved in the shape of animals, birds, or snakes. Lizards are the favorite and most common animal. The head is at one end, and a carved cup for the pieces captured by the leading player is at the opposite end. The pieces are usually dried seeds about the size of marbles. *Ma kpon* is often played outdoors by scooping holes in dirt or sand and using pebbles or shells as pieces.

Won-Ldy describes the rules like this. (1) Start with 4 seeds, small pebbles, or shells in each of the 12 holes. Each player can only move pieces from 1 of the 6 holes on his or her side. Players capture seeds on their opponent's side of the board. They agree where their captured seeds will be kept. One player uses the container at the end of the board and the other player can use a small basket or pot. (2) For the first 2 turns only, each player moves the seeds from any one of his holes and deposits them in any way he wishes in the other holes on his side of the board. This is called "building forts." (This rule makes *ma kpon* more interesting because each game always begins differently.) (3) After the first 4 moves (2 turns for each player), players take turns re-

Dan children playing ma kpon.

moving all of the seeds from 1 of their 6 holes and dropping 1 seed into each of the other 11 holes until they run out of seeds, moving around the board clockwise. (4) Players capture an opponent's seeds by dropping their seeds in an opponent's hole which has less than 2 seeds already in it. The player then takes all the seeds in that hole (including the seed he just dropped in), unless the hole is directly behind a "fort," which is a hole with more than 3 pieces in it. (So it is good strategy to keep at least 3 seeds in as many holes as you can to "protect" them, and the pieces in the holes just behind them, from being captured.) (5) The game ends when one person is out of seeds, but both players must move so that the other person has seeds to play, if they can. (6) The winner is the player who captured the most seeds.

Nimba Mountain Range: Mountains that lie along Liberia's northeastern border, in the part of Liberia that bulges out toward Guinea and the Ivory Coast. Long ridges and dome-shaped hills characterize the Nimba Mountains, which are rich in iron ore, Liberia's most important export. The highest point in Liberia is the Nimba Mountain Range's Guest House Hill at 4,500 feet (1,372 meters).

Palm Nuts: Oil palm trees (not to be confused with coconut palm trees) grow naturally in the forests of Liberia. Dan children climb the trees, using bamboo ladders, to harvest the palm nuts. The nuts are bright red, about the size of walnuts, and grow packed tightly together in bunches. Large bunches can have up to 500 palm nuts and weigh up to 200 pounds (91 kilograms). The children cut the bunches apart into smaller pieces and carry them back to their village in baskets made of sturdy palm leaves. The nuts are boiled to soften the outer shells and make them spongy. The nuts are then pounded to separate the kernels from the shells. The spongy shells are boiled separately from the kernels. The shells release red oil which is skimmed off the water and stored in jars. It remains liquid even when cooled. The kernels release white oil, which hardens when cooled into a white paste the consistency of shortening. Both kinds of oil are used for cooking, skin lotion, hair cream, and wood polish. Extra oil is sold or traded.

Pepper Bird: A grayish bird a little smaller than a crow. Pepper birds are usually the first birds heard early in the morning. They are called pepper birds because they like to eat peppers.

Sankpah (san-kpah´): A drum carved out of wood with a deer hide top. A metal rattle, which vibrates when the drum is played, is attached to the side of the drum. Sankpah come in different sizes, but instead of referring to them as small, medium, and large, they are called child, mother, and father drums. The child drums are usually played by children, and the mother and father drums, which can be up to 15 inches (38 centimeters) in diameter and up to 2 feet (61 centimeters) high, are usually played by adults.

Tapita (ta´-pe-ta): One of the largest Dan towns in Liberia. It is located in the foothills of the Nimba Mountains and is surrounded by rainforest. Most of the residents of Tapita are farmers who grow rice and cassava. Tapita is located at the crossing of two of the most important roads in Liberia—the road that runs east from Monrovia, the capital of Liberia, to the Ivory Coast, and the road that runs south from Guinea to the coastal port of Buchanan. Tapita is one of the political centers of the Dan community. It is especially busy on Wednesdays, the biggest market day.

Tlo Ker Mehn (tro´ ka men): Means "a person who plays story" in the Dan language. A *tlo ker mehn* is a master performer who has a wide variety of specialized skills, all of which are used to enhance his or her storytelling abilities. In addition to knowledge of and expertise in telling the stories, a *tlo ker mehn* is usually a skilled musician, a trained dancer, an experienced actor, and has other complementary skills as well. A *tlo ker mehn* is also a historian, an educator, a politician, and an entertainer. When it becomes known that a *tlo ker mehn* will be at a festival or community activity, everyone looks forward to the event. A *tlo ker mehn* always attracts a crowd.

Won-Yen (waa-nyehn): The younger brother of Won-Ldy. Won-Yen is a fine storyteller and a great singer. Won-Ldy and Won-Yen spent a lot of time while they were growing up telling stories to one another and performing together.

Bibliography

Fischer, Eberhard, and Hans Himmelheber. *The Arts of the Dan in West Africa*. Zürich, Switzerland: Museum Rietberg Zürich, 1984.

Hopson, Dr. Darlene Powell, Dr. Derek S. Hopson, with Thomas Clavin. *Juba This and Juba That: 100 African-American Games for Children*. New York: Simon and Schuster, 1996.

Johnson, Barbara C. *Four Dan Sculptors: Continuity and Change*. San Francisco: The Fine Arts Museum of San Francisco, 1986.

Nelson, Harold D., ed. *Liberia: A Country Study*. Washington D.C.: U.S. Government Printing Office, 1985.

Paye, Won-Ldy, and Margaret H. Lippert, ed. "Why Leopard Has Black Spots: A Story from the Dan People of Liberia." In *Teacher's Read-Aloud Anthology*, Grade 1. Margaret H. Lippert, anthologist. New York: Macmillan/McGraw-Hill School Publishing, 1993, pages 88–92.

About the Authors and Illustrator

Won-Ldy Paye (pronounced One Day Pay) is a member of the Dan ethnic group from Tapita, in the northeastern region of Liberia. His family are the *tlo ker mehn*, or storytellers, of the Dan community. Won-Ldy was trained by his grandmother to remember and retell the stories of the Dan people.

In Liberia, Won-Ldy was a performer and a director. One of the plays he directed won an international award. He founded and directed a theater company, which became the fourth largest in Liberia.

Now Won-Ldy lives in Seattle where he teaches Liberian arts in schools and Liberian drumming and dance at the University of Washington. He directs a group of Liberian

Photo by Mike McClure

musicians and masked dancers, which performs at community events and festivals. Won-Ldy plays various instruments including *sankpah* and *balaphone*. Since 1990 he has hosted a weekly radio program that focuses on African issues and culture.

Won-Ldy's colorful and dramatic paintings hang in private collections on the East Coast and in California. He dyes fabric and makes clothes in the Dan style for himself and his friends, and his backyard is full of drums in all stages of construction.

Won-Ldy maintains close ties with his friends and family in Liberia. He lives with his daughter, Kerlia, and his son, Nlorkeahwon, who have also had the opportunity to learn the traditional Dan arts from their grandparents in Liberia.

Margaret (Meg) Lippert grew up outside Philadelphia in a cooperative community of several hundred acres where 60 families of different cultures and religions worked together to clear land, build homes, maintain roads, grow food, and live in harmony with one another. She continues telling the stories she learned from her Irish grandmother and her English father. Meg worked for a year in Tanzania and a year in Guatemala, where she learned many more stories.

Meg was an elementary school teacher and founded and directed a non-graded elementary school. She taught children's literature at Teacher's College, Columbia University, and storytelling at Bank Street College of Education. Her 18 books include *Why the Moon Is in the Sky*, illustrated

Photo by Peggy Jarrell Kaplan

by Leo and Diane Dillon (Macmillan, 1988), and a 9-volume *Teacher's Read Aloud Anthology* of multicultural stories for grades K through 8 (Macmillan/McGraw-Hill School Publishing, 1993). *The Sea Serpent's Daughter: A Brazilian Legend,* illustrated by Felipe Davalos (Troll, 1993), is available in Spanish as *La Hija de la Serpiente Marina. Finist the Falcon: A Russian Legend,* illustrated by Dave Albers (Troll, 1996), was inspired by her daughter's visit to Russia in 1995.

Meg has traveled from coast to coast and to Canada and Europe telling stories and giving workshops for teachers. She lives with her family on Mercer Island near Seattle. Her daughters, Jocelyn and Dawn, are accomplished storytellers and often perform with her.

Ashley Bryan was born in Harlem and grew up in The Bronx. His first books were illustrated ABC and counting books that he made in kindergarten. He was educated at the Cooper Union Art School and Columbia University. Even in the army in France during World War II he continued to sketch, keeping his drawing paper dry in his gas mask pack.

Photo by Matthew Wysocki

After the war he returned to Europe on a Fulbright scholarship to study art in France and Germany. His visits to Africa inspired him to retell and illustrate the African folktales for which he is so well known, including *Beat the Story Drum, Pum-Pum* (Coretta Scott King Award for Illustration) and *Lion and Ostrich Chicks* (Coretta Scott King Honor Book). His West Indian folktale, *The Cat's Purr,* and his collections of Black American Spirituals, *Walk Together Children* and *I'm Going to Sing,* were ALA Notable

Children's Books. In 1990 he received the Arbuthnot Prize, a prestigious international award given to recognize lifetime achievement in children's literature.

For many years he taught art at Dartmouth College. He currently travels throughout the world captivating audiences of adults and children with his powerful storytelling and poetry presentations. When he is not traveling, he lives on an island off the coast of Maine where he paints, makes puppets from objects he finds as he walks along the beach, creates stained-glass windows from beach glass, and writes and illustrates books. His recent books include *Sing to the Sun* (Parents' Choice Award 1992), an illustrated collection of his own poetry, and *Ashley Bryan's ABC of African-American Poetry* (1997). Two video documentaries feature his life and work: the National Geographic production "Island Storyteller" made in 1984 and American School Publishers' "Meet Ashley Bryan: Storyteller, Artist, Writer" made in 1992.